Philipp Winterberg

FiFTEEN FEET OF TiME

Pet Metara od Vremena

English [US] (English)
Bosnian (Bosanski)

Translation (English): Christina Riesenweber, Japhet Johnstone and EUP Team
Translation (Bosnian): Meliha Fazlic, Iliriana Bisha Tagani and and EUP Team

www.philippwinterberg.com

Idea/Illustrations: Lena Hesse · Text: Lena Hesse, Philipp Winterberg · Fonts: Lena Hesse, Patua One, Noto Sans, etc. · Photos: Philipp Winterberg, etc. · Originally published in Germany as *Fünf Meter Zeit* by Lena Hesse and Philipp Winterberg, Münster, in 2007. Copyright © 2007 Lena Hesse, Philipp Winterberg · Publisher/Copyright © 2021 Philipp Winterberg, Graelstraße 37, D-48153 Münster, www.philippwinterberg.com · All rights reserved. No part of this book may be reproduced, stored in a retrieval system, or transmitted by any means without the written permission of the publisher.

The story that I want to tell you happened not too long ago in a city so big that it takes many days if you try to cross it by bike. Even by car it takes several hours.

Priča koju želim da vam ispričam dogodila se ne tako davno, u tako velikom gradu da je potrebno mnogo dana ako ga pokušate prijeći biciklom. Čak i sa automobilom potrebno je nekoliko sati.

This city is crammed full of life. Life that walks and stands and crawls, strolls, creeps, jumps and sometimes even flies. Nobody knows how many people exactly are living in this city, but there might be about seven and onety three quarter phantastillion ten and one billion gillion tweleven million hundred and twenty-four thousand three hundred forty-eight and eleven.

There is rarely a house that does not have at least twenty stories to accommodate all the people of the city.

And when you walk the streets of the city, the dizzy buzz of noises becomes so loud from time to time that you have to cover your ears for a bit to clear your head again.

Ovaj grad je prepun života. Života koji hoda i stoji, puže, šeta, skače a ponekad čak i leti. Niko ne zna koliko ljudi zapravo živi u ovom gradu, ali vjeruje se da žive oko deset triliona, pet biliona i trista dvadeset i pet miliona i sedamdeset i šest stanovnika.

Rjetka je kuća koja nema najmanje dvadeset spratova, da udomi sve stanovnike ovoga grada.

I kada hodate ulicama ovoga grada, zvukovi i buka postaju toliko glasni da s vremena na vrijeme morate pokriti uši da bi na kratko razbistrili glavu.

In this city, there began a day just like any other, a regular weekday, when most of the people were running errands early in the morning or going to work.

U ovom gradu, počeo je dan baš kao i svaki drugi, običan radni dan, u
kojem je većina ljudi trčala rano ujutro za obavezama ili na posao.

It must have been about seven a.m., when a small and slightly
hunch-backed snail was standing at a crosswalk.

Mora da je bilo oko sedam ujutro, kada je mali grbavi puž
stajao na zebri.

It first looked to the right ... ... and then to the left ...
... and just to be sure also up ... ... and down.
You never know.

Prvo je pogledao desno ... ... pa onda lijevo ...

... i da bude sasvim siguran, pogledao je i gore ... ... i dole.

Nikada se ne zna.

... and after it had convinced itself that all cars were still quite far away, it started its journey. And as it is common among all snaily creatures, it was moving incredibly ………
…………s…………………l………………………o……………………………………………
.w………………………………………………………………l…………………………………y……………

It hadn't even moved three inches by the time everybody else had already crossed the street and disappeared into the bustling crowds on the other side. The first cars came, some with silently squeaking tires, to a halt in front of the crosswalk.

I know what you're expecting now: people checking their wristwatches in annoyance, noisy complaints, long blasts of honking, maybe some random ruffian picking up the little snail to carry it to the other side of the street hastily, so that things could ***moveonfinallymoveon!*** That's what you're counting on, right?
Nothing like that happened.

… i nakon što se uvjerio da su sva vozila dosta daleko, krenuo je naprijed. I kao što je to uobičajeno za sve pužiće, počeo je da se kreće veoma ………………………………………s…..
…………………p…………………o…………………………r…………………………o………………
Nije prešao ni nekoliko centimentara, a svi drugi već su prešli ulicu i nestali u gužvi na drugoj strani ulice. Prvi automobili su došli, neki i sa gumama koje su škripale do zastoja ispred zebre.

Znam šta vi sada očekujete: ljude koji užurbano gledaju svoje ručne satove, trubanje sirena, i možda neki slučajni prolaznik koji uzima puža i nosi ga ljutito do drugog kraja ulice, kako bi on napokon mogao da nastavi svoj put!
To je ono na šta vi očekujete, zar ne?
Ništa od toga se nije desilo.

In a van that had stopped right in front of the crosswalk, there was a small tree frog. His job was to forecast the weather every day (once in the morning at six, then again at seven thirty, at noon and then again at eight in the evening).

He was the only weather-frog far and wide, and this is why he was broadcast on every TV channel in the city. The frog was about to honk his horn – considering that it was seven already and his next forecast was coming up in half an hour – when he saw, in his rear-view mirror, how behind him the sun was rising slowly and bathing all of the houses one by one in golden light.

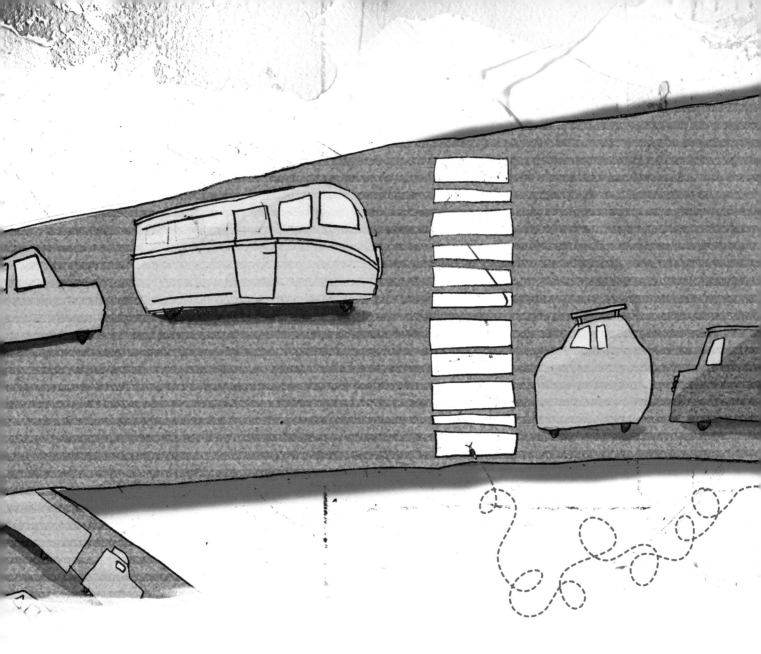

U kombiju koji je stao ispred zebre, nalazio se maleni žabac. Njegov posao je bio da prognozira vrijeme svaki dan (jednom ujutro u šest sati, pa ponovo u sedam i trideset, u podne i onda opet još jednom u osam naveče).

On je bio jedini žabac-meteorolog na cijelom tom prostoru, i to je razlog zašto je emitovan na svakom TV kanalu u gradu. Žabac je upravo htio da zatrubi sirenu- s obzirom na to da je već sedam sati i njegova slijedeća prognoza je za pola sata - kada je primjetio, u njegovom retrovizoru, kako se sunce iza njega polako diže i prekriva sve kuće jednu po jednu zlatnim svjetlom.

He frowned and thought to himself: I'm always talking about the weather. And I've been doing this for so long now that I can't even recall the last time that I actually felt and enjoyed the weather. After all, there is no weather in the weather studio.

He sat like that for a moment and then he turned off the engine of his van, got out and grabbed his weather-frog ladder to climb on to the roof of a house.

And he picked the highest one in the street.

Žabac tuzno pomisli u sebi: Ja uvjek govorim samo o vremenu. Radim ovaj posao već tako dugo da se ne mogu više ni sjetiti kada sam zadnji put stvarno uživao u lijepom vremenu. U studiju nikada ne vidim kakvo je zaista vrijeme vani.

Sjedio je tako neko vrijeme i napokon isključio motor svoga kombija, izašao vani te uzeo svoje merdevine i popeo se na krov jedne kuće.

Izabrao je najvišu kuću u toj ulici.

About the same time, an Italian violin that was famous well beyond the city limits, got out of her limousine and asked the driver to help her get on the roof of the car so that everybody would see her.

'Signorina,' the driver piped up, 'The rehearsal at the Philharmonic!' The violin wasn't worried. 'At the Philharmonic, there are only empty rows of chairs at this point of the day. Some musically challenged mice at best! But look around you – this place is full of people! There is no place nicer to play than this!'

U isto vrijeme, jedna italijanska violina veoma poznata i dalje od grada, izašla je iz svoje limuzine i zamolila je šofera da joj pomogne da se popne na krov od automobila kako bi je svi vidjeli.

"Sinjorina" reče šofer "..Proba u Filharmoniji!?" Violina nije bila zabrinuta. "Trenutno su u Filharmoniji samo prazni redovi i stolice. Moguće neki slabo muzički talentovani miševi!" "Ali pogledaj oko sebe – ovo mjesto je prepuno ljudi. Nema boljeg mjesta za sviranje od ovoga!"

As she stood on the roof, she curtsied and began to play for all the waiting people.
And even though the song was very new (it wasn't to premiere until a week later and
she still needed some practice) everybody was enchanted. They closed their eyes
and listened in awe.

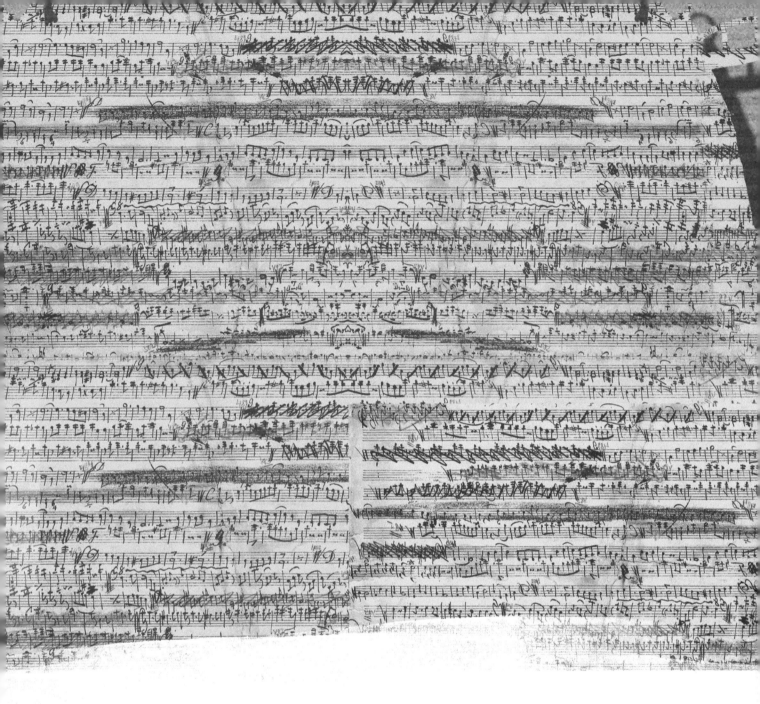

I tako, dok je stajala na krovu, ona se nakloni i poče da svira za sve ljude koji su čekali. Iako je pjesma bila potpuno nova (premijera je bila zakazana za sedam dana kasnije, a i njoj je trebalo još malo prakse) svi su se očarali. Zatvorili su oči i slušali muziku s'poštovanjem.

There was a scuttling in an alley. A scuttling the likes of which can only come from a many-legged creature. It was the cross spider who usually is never seen during daylight. Mostly, she spent nights annoying the tenants of the house by weaving her threads across their windows and doors and even across the street to make people trip. But now, to everybody's surprise, she lowered herself from a drainpipe and listened with half-closed eyes to the music of the famous Italian violin.

Then she picked up two long, thin sticks and started – her eyes still halfway closed – knitting.

U tim trenutcima, došlo je do neke buke u obližnoj uličici. Buka koju jedino može stvoriti nego stvorenje sa mnogo nogu. Bio je to pauk koji obično spava u ovo doba dana. Uglavnom, on provodi dane u kućama stanara, plečući mreže preko njihovih vrata i prozora, a i preko ulice kako bi se ljudi u to upletali. Ali sada, na iznenađenje mnogih, spustio se iz oluka i slušao poluzatvorenih očiju muziku čuvene italijanske violine.

Zatim je pokupio dva duga, tanka štapića i počeo – sa očima još uvijek na pola zatvorenim - da plete.

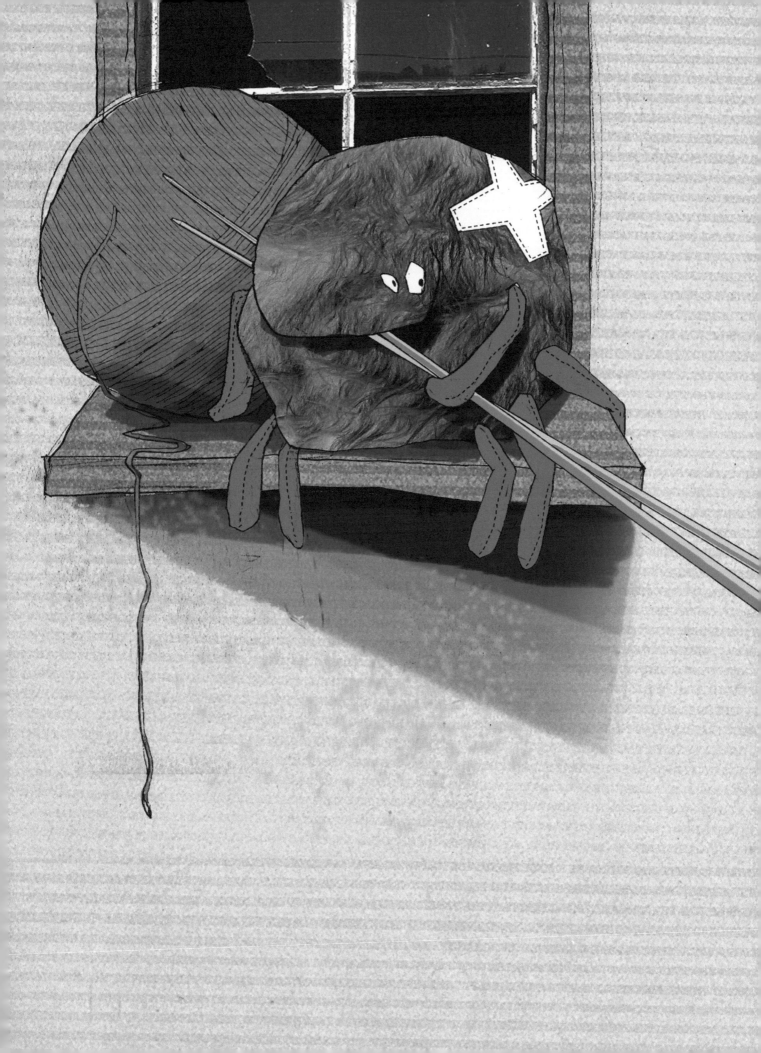

'What are you knitting? A scarf?' two penguins called up to the spider
 from the windows of their car.

'It is still way too hot for a scarf,' replied the spider in a friendly tone.

'I'm not quite sure what it's gonna be.'

The penguins consulted with each other briefly.

'Make a hammock!' one of them shouted.

'Yes, a hammock!' the other one backed him up. And both climbed out
 of their car and waddled awkwardly up to the spider.

'For the both of us!' they called out. 'So we can put it up over the street
 and sit in it! And listen to the violin play and enjoy the sun!'

"Šta pleteš? Šal?", dva pingvina upitaše pauka sa prozora svog automobila.

"Još uvijek je previše toplo za šal.", odgovori pauk prijateljski.

"Nisam sasvim siguran šta će to zapravo biti."

Pingvini porazgovaraše međusobno na kratko.

"Napravi ležaljku!" odgovori jedan pingvin.

"Da ležaljku!" podrža ga drugi.

Te obojica izađoše iz svog automobila i krenuše se gegati ka pauku.

"Za nas oboje!" odgovariše. "Dakle, možemo ga staviti preko ulice i sjediti u ležaljci!
Slušati violinu kako svira i uživati na suncu!"

And after a little pause one said to the other:
'And maybe we can play some cards.'
'We could play cards!' the other one shouted
to the spider and explained:
'You know, we work at the casino and there we can only
watch other people play. We're just the card dealers!'
'Croupiers,' the other whispered to him.
'Croupiers!' the first one corrected himself and then
said, facing the spider:
'Will you knit a hammock for us?'

The spider smiled a friendly smile.

Nakon kratke pauze drugi reče: "Možemo se igrati
i karata."
"Mogli bismo se kartati!" reče drugi uzbuđeno
pauku i objasni:
"Znate, mi radimo u kasinu i tu možemo samo
gledati druge ljude kako igraju. Mi samo
djelimo karte!"
"Krupieri!", šapnu drugi.
"Krupieri!" prvi ispravi sebe, a onda reče:
"Hoćeš li plesti ležaljku za nas?"

Pauk se nasmješi.

Because spiders know how to work threads very well, it wasn't long before the two penguins were taking off their starched tuxedos and cozying up in a big hammock, made out of soft spider wool.

While the weather-frog was sitting in the sun, and while the violin was fiddling, and while the spider was knitting, and while the penguins were playing Go Fish and Rummy, at the crosswalk, in the third row, the door of a red truck opened and a gargoyle hopped out.

Zato što pauci znaju vrlo dobro kako se plete, ne prođe dugo i dva pingvina su skinula
njihova uštirkana odjela i raskomotili se u velikoj ležaljci, napravljenoj od mekane vune.

Dok je žabac meteorolog uživao na suncu, i dok je violina svirala, i dok je pauk pleo, i dok
su pingvini igrali se sa kartama, na zebri, u trećem redu, vrata jednog crvenog kamiona se
otvoriše i jedan gargol iskoči vani.

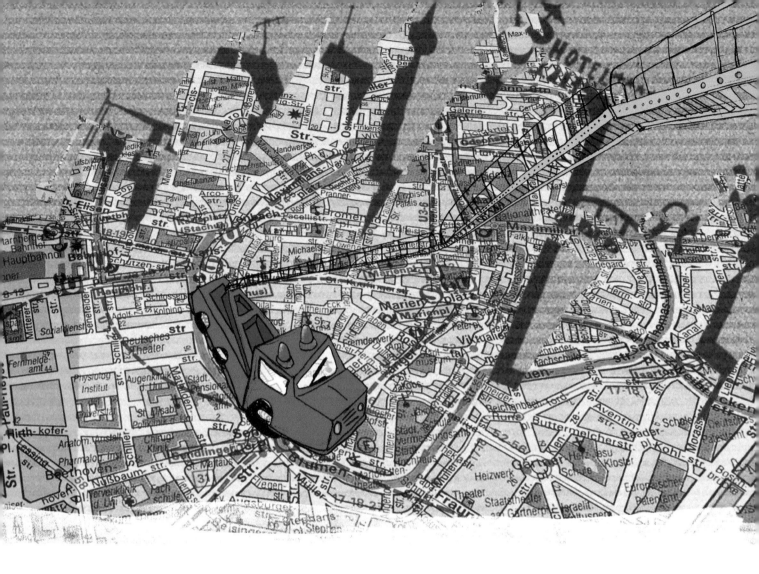

From the outside, gargoyles don't look much different from average dragons, but instead of fire they breathe – you guessed it: *water*.

Because of this special ability they usually work with the fire department. Therefore, nobody was surprised to see that this particular gargoyle was traveling in a fire truck. With a steady hand he extended the metal ladder that was part of the truck. 'What are you up to?' somebody asked him – because there didn't appear to be a fire anywhere nearby or a kitten stuck in a tree.

Gargoli se ne razlikavaju mnogo od drugih zmajeva, ali umjesto vatre oni
pušu – šta mislis? Tako je: *vodu*.

Zbog ove posebne sposobnosti oni obično rade sa vatrogascima.
Dakle, niko nije bio iznenađen da vidi da je baš ovaj gargol putovao
u vatrogasnom kamionu. On mirno rasklopi metalne merdevine
koje su bile dio kamiona.
"Šta to nameravaš?", neko ga upita – jer nije izgledalo je je neki
požar u blizini ili da se neko mače zaglavilo na drvetu.

'I stand on this ladder all the time, but I've never actually considered for a single moment just enjoying the beautiful view!' said the gargoyle with a grin.
Then he started his climb.

And when he saw the big city spread out below him in the warm sunlight, he was so full of joy that he made a big cloud of shiny bubbles that floated gently to the ground and burst with a barely audible ... *POP*.

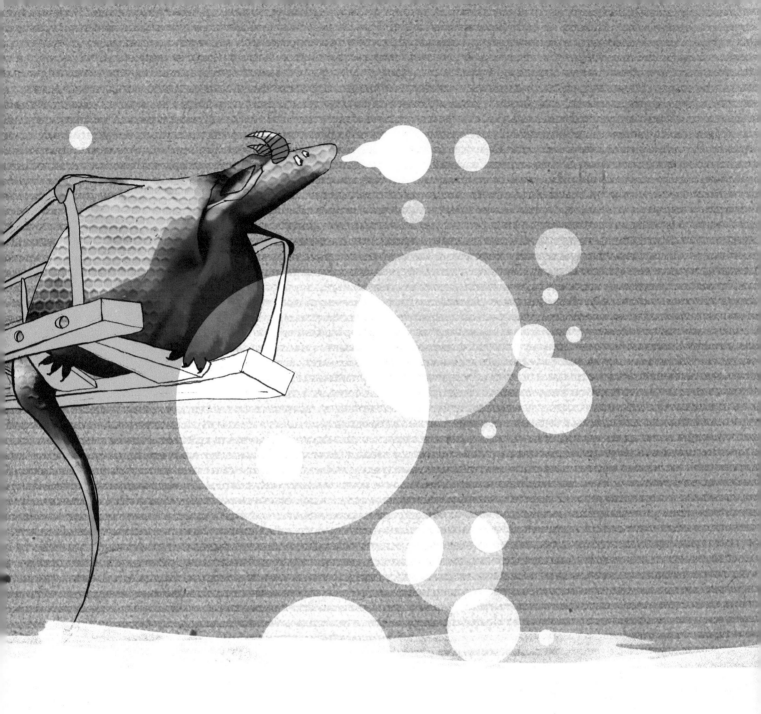

"Ja stalno stojim na ovim merdevinama, ali nikada se nisam popeo samo da uživam u predivnom pogledu!", reče gargol sa osmjehom, te poče da se penje.

I kada je vidio veliki grad kako se rasuo ispod njega, u toplom suncu, bio je pun radosti da je napravio veliki oblak sjajnih mjehurića koji su plutali nježno ka zemlji i tiho pucketali ... *POP*.

Many hours later, when the little snail had finally reached the other side of the street, the twilight of night was already approaching.

'Good to see you – I've just arrived, too!' the rabbit greeted. He had been waiting for the snail leaning against a light post.
'What should we do? Are you hungry?'

Mnogo sati kasnije, kada je napokon mali pužić stigao na drugi kraj ulice, mrak je počeo da pada.

"Drago mi je što te vidim – i ja sam tek stigao!" pozdravi ga zec. On je čekao pužića naslonjen na javnu rasvjetu.
"Šta da radimo sada? Jesi li gladan?"

'And how!' the snail sighed and its gaze turned all dreamy at the thought of fresh lettuce.

'I've been traveling for quite a while ...'

The weather frog decided to drive back to the TV studio once again to make the last weather forecast of the day. The next day would be sunny, he knew that. After all, he had been watching the sky all day. For the first time, he thought, I have the feeling that I actually know what I'm talking about.

"I te kako!" odgovori puž zamislivši svježu glavicu kupusa.

"Putovao sam već neko vrijeme ....."

Žaba meteorolog odluči da vozi natrag u TV studio da obavi posljednju vremensku prognozu za taj dan. Sutra će biti sunčano, on je već znao. Na kraju krajeva, gledao je u nebo cijeli dan. Po prvi put, pomislio je, imam osjećaj da zapravo znam šta pričam.

Everybody else who had been waiting now continued on their way, filled with happiness from the sun, the music, and the bubbles. Some were carrying hammocks or clothes under their arms that the spider had made for them. The two casino penguins collected their playing cards, slipped back into their elegant tuxedos and gave their spot in the hammock over to the fat cross spider. She made herself cozy there and – tired from all her new impressions of the city in the daylight – fell asleep happily.

Svi ostali koji su čekali sada su nastavili svoj put, ispunjeni srećom od sunca, muzikom, i mjehurićima. Neki su nosili ležaljke ili odjeću ispod ruke, ležaljke i odjeću koju je pauk ispleo za njih. Dva kasino pingvina prikupili su svoje karte, obukli opet svoja elegantna odjela i dali svoje mjesto u ležaljci debelom pauku. On se lijepo raskomotio - umoran od novih utisaka grada tokom dana – te je veseo zaspao.

THE END

Philipp B. Winterberg M.A. studied
Communication Science, Psychology and
Law. He lives in Berlin and loves being
multifaceted: He went parachuting in
Namibia, meditated in Thailand, and swam
with sharks and stingrays
in Fiji and Polynesia.

Philipp Winterberg's books introduce
new perspectives on essential themes like
friendship, mindfulness and happiness. They
are read in languages and countries all over
the globe.

CPSIA information can be obtained
at www.ICGtesting.com
Printed in the USA
BVHW020059181121
621914BV00001B/9